OXFORD GRADE[
500 Headwords

Goldilocks
and the Three Bears

OXFORD UNIVERSITY PRESS

Oxford University Press, Walton Street, Oxford OX2 6DP

OXFORD NEW YORK
ATHENS AUCKLAND BANGKOK BOMBAY
CALCUTTA CAPE TOWN DAR ES SALAAM DELHI
FLORENCE HONG KONG ISTANBUL KARACHI
KUALA LUMPUR MADRAS MADRID MELBOURNE
MEXICO CITY NAIROBI PARIS SINGAPORE
TAIPEI TOKYO TORONTO

and associated companies in
BERLIN IBADAN

OXFORD and OXFORD ENGLISH are
trade marks of Oxford University Press

ISBN 0 19 421703 5

© *Oxford University Press 1971*

First published 1971
Tenth impression 1994

Goldilocks and the Three Bears is written by L.A. Hill
The illustrations are by Prudence Seward.

No unauthorized photocopying

Printed in Hong Kong

1 Goldilocks

Goldilocks was a small girl. Her father's house was near a forest.

Her mother said, 'Do not go into the forest, Goldilocks. There are bad animals there.' Goldilocks said, 'Yes, Mother,' and she did not go into the forest.

Goldilocks is older now. She is eight years old. She is looking at the forest, and she is saying, 'There are some beautiful flowers near the side of the forest. I am going to cut some, and I am going to take them to Mother.'

She took her mother's basket, and she went to the forest.

2 The Flowers in the Forest

Goldilocks was near the forest. She said, 'The flowers under those trees are more beautiful,' and she went to them. She cut them, and she put them in her basket.

Then there were some blue flowers, and then there were some big, red ones. Goldilocks was in the forest now.

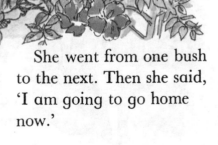

She went from one bush to the next. Then she said, 'I am going to go home now.'

But where was her house? She was afraid.

Then she looked at some
big trees, and she smiled.
She said, 'Those trees
are near our house.'
She went to them—but
her house was not behind
them. They were like the
trees near her house, but
they were not those trees.

3 The House in
   the Forest

Goldilocks shouted, but there were not any people
in the forest. Then she cried, because she was
afraid. Were there any animals there?
She walked, and she ran, and then she walked
again,

and she came to a small house.

The door was open, but she knocked at it. Then she knocked again.

Then she said, 'The house is empty.'

She walked in, and she went to the kitchen. There were three bowls of porridge on the table. One of them was big, one of them was middle-sized, and one of them was small.

Goldilocks was hungry.
She took a spoonful of
porridge from the big
bowl, and she put it in her
mouth, but there was a lot
of salt in it. She said,
'This is not good porridge.'

Then she took some
porridge from the
middle-sized bowl. There
was not any sugar in it.
Goldilocks said, 'This is
bad porridge too.'

Then she took some
porridge from the small
bowl. It was sweet, and
there was a little salt
in it too.

Goldilocks said, 'This is
very good porridge,' and
she ate all of it.

7

4 The Three Chairs

Then Goldilocks went to the living-room. There were three chairs in it. One of them was big, one of them was middle-sized, and one of them was small.

Goldilocks was tired. She sat on the big chair, but it was very hard. She said, 'This is not a good chair.'

She went to the middle-sized chair, and she sat on that, but it was very soft.
She said, 'This is a bad chair too.'

Then she went to the small chair. It was not very hard, and it was not very soft.

Goldilocks looked at it. Then she said, 'This is a good chair. I am going to sit on this one.'

She sat on it, but it was a weak chair, and she was a heavy girl. The chair broke, and Goldilocks fell on the floor.

5 The Three Beds

Then she went upstairs. There were three bedrooms there. There was a big bed in the first one, there was a middle-sized bed in the second one, and there was a small bed in the third one.

Goldilocks lay on the first bed. It was very hard.

She went to the second bedroom, and she lay on the middle-sized bed, but it was very soft.

She went to the third bedroom, and she lay on the small bed. It was very good, and she said, 'I am going to sleep here, because I am very tired. Then I am going to go home.'

6 The Three Bears

The house was a bears' house. They were in the forest, because it was a sunny day. They came home at midday, and they went into their house.

They went to the kitchen, and they looked at their porridge. The father bear said, 'Who has eaten some of my porridge?'

Then the mother bear said, 'And who has eaten some of my porridge?'

But the baby bear cried, and he said, 'Who has eaten all of my porridge?'

Then the three bears went into their living-room, and the father bear said, 'Who has sat in my chair?'

The mother bear said, 'And who has sat in my chair?'

But the baby bear cried again, and he said, 'Who has broken my chair?'

Then the three bears went upstairs.

The father bear looked at his bed, and he said, 'Who has lain on my bed?'

The mother bear looked at her bed, and she said, 'And who has lain on my bed?'

But the baby bear looked at his bed, and he said, 'And who is lying in my bed?'

Goldilocks was asleep, but she woke up. She looked at the three bears, and she was very afraid.

7 Home Again

She jumped out of the
baby bear's bed. She ran
downstairs. She ran out of
the house, and she ran
into the forest.

She ran, and then she walked, and then she ran
again,

and she came to the side of the forest.
Her house was in front of
her. She was very happy.
She ran in, and she did not
go into the forest again.

forest

This is a **forest**. There are a lot of trees in a **forest**.

lying/lay/lain

Peter is **lying** on the floor.

Helen **lay** on her bed yesterday afternoon.

John has **lain** on some mud. His back is muddy.

middle-sized   Not small, and not big.

This bear is big,   this one is small,   and this one is **middle-sized**.

porridge

George is having breakfast.

He is putting sugar on his **porridge.**

Now he is eating it.

woke

Sally was asleep at eight o'clock.

She **woke** at half past eight.

Now she is awake.

1. Where did Goldilocks live?
2. Why did her mother say, 'Do not go into the forest'?
3. What did Goldilocks cut in the forest?
4. Why did Goldilocks go to the big trees? Were they the right trees?
5. What did she do then?
6. Was there anybody in the small house?
7. She did not eat the porridge in the big bowl. Why?
8. And she did not eat the porridge in the middle-sized bowl. Why?
9. Why did she eat the porridge in the small bowl?
10. Why did she sit on the small chair?
11. She did not sleep on the big bed, and she did not sleep on the middle-sized one. Why?
12. Whose house was Goldilocks in?
13. Why is the small bear crying in the top picture on page 12?
14. Goldilocks did not go into the forest again. Why?

Put a basket in
Goldilocks' hand.

Draw the three
bowls of porridge
on this table.

Draw the baby
bear's bed.

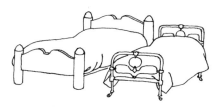

Put these words in the empty holes:

is going to pick	is picking	picked
is going to knock	is knocking	knocked
is going to eat	is eating	ate
is going to sit	is sitting	sat

Goldilocks . . . . . . some
flowers yesterday.
She . . . . . . some now.
She . . . . . . some
tomorrow.

Goldilocks . . . . . . some
porridge yesterday.
She . . . . . . some now.
She . . . . . . some
tomorrow.

Goldilocks . . . . . . at
this door yesterday.
She . . . . . . at it now.
She . . . . . . at it
tomorrow.

Goldilocks . . . . . . on the
baby bear's chair yesterday.
She . . . . . . on it now.
She . . . . . . on it
tomorrow.